Camp Century

CHRISTOFFER PETERSEN

Camp Century

By Christoffer Petersen

AARLUUK PRESS

Christoffer Petersen has asserted his right under the Copyright, Designs and Patents Act 1988 to be identified as the author of this work.

ISBN: 978-87-93680-77-7

www.christoffer-petersen.com

Part 1

It's hard to imagine a typical journalistic assignment in Greenland, and, as experience has shown, there is often a crime associated with each of them. Why then should a geological field trip to Camp Century prove any different? Of course, I knew it wasn't a run-of-the-mill geology expedition, there were far too many colourful characters in the mix, including the technical advisor, Arika Jones, chosen for her knowledge of glaciers and ice, but none the less interesting for her Australian Aboriginal background. I could write a whole article just about her. But my editor wanted more than a personal profile piece. He said there was something strange about the expedition, that when he saw the list of expedition members, he just knew something was going on. I had to admit, the American historian in his fifties, together with his Greenlandic companion, piqued my interest. The fact that they went missing on the third day after their arrival at camp just added to the intrigue. That was when Arika took over.

"It's likely," she said, "that they have fallen down a crevasse. Lærke has organised the teams for the search."

I shuffled my feet in the snow as Lærke Toft Hansen, the Danish leader of the geology expedition, took a step forward. She ran a gloved finger down a list of names tacked to an old-fashioned clipboard, calling out the leaders before assigning two more people to each team.

"I realise we're still getting to know each other," she said, brushing her grey fringe to one side. "So, it makes sense just to remind you who we're looking for." She hugged the clipboard to her chest, pressing the air out of her thick winter jacket, and said, "Most of you know Josh Shellenberger." She paused at a quick wave of smiles that spread between the expedition members – twelve in all, including me, but minus Josh and his companion. "Josh is our resident historian, and I know he has entertained many of you with his Camp Century stories on the flight up here. But you might not have met his companion, Serminnguaq Satorana. She joined us at Thule Air Base. Both of them are in their fifties. And now, obviously," she said, with a nod to the group assembled in front of her, "they are missing. It might be they just went for a walk…"

"And broke the first rule of camp," Arika said. "No-one leaves camp without permission and they can only get that by signing out with either Lærke or me in the main tent."

It struck me that Arika was perfect for the job of safety advisor, but I did wonder if she was capable of relaxing, and how she would react when the expedition members actually started to venture beyond the camp perimeter.

"Yes," Lærke said. "But if they have just gone for a walk, then I'm hoping they haven't gone far."

"They don't need to go far to get into trouble," Arika said. "This area is riddled with crevasses, and

God knows what else," she said, fiddling with the film badge dosimeter hanging from a lanyard around her neck.

I checked my own badge and wondered just how much radiation was too much and how I would even know? I had missed Josh Shellenberger's impromptu talk about radioactive waste from Camp Century. One of the younger members of the expedition had put him on the spot. But I remembered Arika's comments about shifting ice, and how the waste had been spread over a massive area since the reactor was removed in 1967. I looked at my feet. I could be standing on top of radioactive waste without even knowing it. Arika's voice dragged me back to the job at hand as she checked everyone's climbing harness, the ropes connecting each team, and the ice axes we carried.

"You're a journalist?" she said, as she tugged at the loop at the front of my harness.

"Yes."

"Danish?"

"Yes."

"Your government has been awfully quiet about this, hasn't it?"

"You mean the radiation?"

"I mean the camp, the radiation, the lack of clean-up, the deniability – yes," she said. "I mean all of those things."

"Well," I said, wondering where to start.

"Are you going to write about it?"

"I'm going to write about something. That *is* why I'm here."

Arika stopped fussing for a second and stared

into my eyes. I had never met an Australian Aboriginal before, but despite being wrapped up in high-tech climbing equipment, including a shapely short-waisted winter jacket with a high collar, Arika seemed to radiate something of the desert, together with a passion for the land. The thick black curls of her hair escaping from the fleece hat sitting snug on her head, bobbed as she sniffed in the cold, before tapping me on the shoulder so that she could check the back of my harness.

"I don't like having civilians on an expedition," she said. Her fingers dug into the back of my thighs as she untwisted one of the leg loops.

"You're a civilian."

"I meant *non-climbers*."

She tapped me again and I turned around. I waited for her to say something more, but she just shook her head.

"Will I do?"

"You'll do," she said. "Just stay with your group."

I watched Arika walk away, crunching the surface layer of snow beneath her winter climbing boots. She was shorter than me, but she walked tall. That was the impression I got. It was the impression she left on everyone, according to the chatter in the camp at night. I shrugged and found my team, letting the leader clip me into the rope that would keep us all secured and stop the *civilians* from wandering off. His face was hidden behind polarised goggles, the kind that reflect a petrol rainbow of colour, but he smiled, and I felt instantly more welcome, despite my lack of climbing experience. I was just about to ask his name, to check if I had remembered correctly. He could have been Brian or Roger. But when someone shouted that they had found Josh, it didn't seem to matter anymore.

The four teams trudged across the ice to a dip just beyond the camp perimeter. The ice flowed in a classic tongue shape down towards the west, its tip curling sharply to the north, revealing a hollow beneath the curl. Lærke called out for everyone to wait, which we didn't, and to be careful, which we weren't. Only Arika's sharp tongue stopped anyone from walking too closely to the body sprawled in the snow ahead of us.

Arika unclipped her safety line and approached the body, one hand on her ice axe, digging it into the surface of the ice with each step. She stuffed the axe into the ice to one side of the body, before she knelt beside it to turn it over.

Even at the distance Arika had us wait I recognised Josh Shellenberger's face, although his cheeks were more flushed than I remembered, as if he had struggled for air during his last moments.

"He's dead," Arika said. She turned to look over her shoulder at Lærke. "You're going to have to call someone."

Lærke nodded. She tugged at the chest pocket of her jacket, her fingers fumbling with the flap and the zip, before she pulled out a satellite phone. "Yes," she said. "Yes, I'll call."

We all watched as she tried to remove her gloves and hold the satellite phone, but even though it was cold, it seemed to me that her fingers were shaking far more than the temperature warranted.

"Let me help you," I said, taking a step forward.

"Wait."

I felt a tug at my waist as Brian – I think that was his name – unclipped my safety line. I nodded my thanks and then strode the last few metres to Lærke.

"I'm sorry," she said. "My fingers..."

"It's all right." I turned the phone in my hand and unlocked the keypad.

"Do you really think he's dead?"

"He looks it," I said. I pulled up the pre-set list of contacts and found the number for the emergency services. "I guess we need the police? If he's dead…"

"He's definitely dead," Arika said. She nodded at the phone in my hand. "You may as well talk to them. You're Danish."

"They speak English," I said, but she had already moved away, drawing Lærke with her. Arika spoke in hushed tones, but I heard words to the effect of *be strong* and *leadership*, and then I decided to make the call.

Once I had explained the situation to the control centre, and they had ascertained that no-one was in danger, and that the victim was indeed dead – Arika confirmed with a sharp nod of her head when I repeated the question in English – they said they would send a local police officer, and that we shouldn't touch the body before they arrived. I confirmed that we would wait in camp, but it never occurred to me that we were still missing one person. The shock of discovering a dead member of the expedition stunned everybody with the same numbing paralysis.

Arika left two people with a radio by Shellenberger's body and herded the rest of us back to camp. It was only when we heard the approach of a helicopter two hours later, that someone remembered that the Greenlandic woman was still missing.

"Oh my God," Lærke said. "What if she's dead, too? I can't cope with that."

The helicopter – an American air force Huey – flared above the area designated as the camp landing pad, marked with oil drums and flags that flapped in the downdraught from the Huey's rotors. Arika raised her hand to protect her face from the swirl of ice that blistered through the air, but I caught a glimpse of the determined set of her jaw. Even in the face of forgetting the missing Greenlander, she still captured the image of the strong leader, quite the opposite from the unassuming face of the police officer who climbed out of the helicopter. He tucked his hands into his jacket pockets as soon as he was clear of the helicopter skids, walking with the quiet confidence that I remembered and looked forward to each time I met Constable David Maratse. He nodded once at me before turning to look at Arika.

"Someone has died?" he said, in his scratchy English.

"Josh Shellenberger," Arika said. "He's fifty-three. American. He's the expedition historian…"

Maratse nodded towards the camp. "Where?"

"Right," she said, and I hid my smile as I

realised it was the very first time she had seemed flustered. She recovered in less than a second, set her jaw to maximum, and pointed to the far side of the camp. "I'll take you there."

I tagged along behind them, wondering when or if Arika would call Maratse a *civilian*, or if locals were exempt? The pilots and crew stayed with their helicopter as we walked through the camp and then up and over the rise that hid Shellenberger's body. Arika led the way, waving the two young geologists away from the body as we approached. She stopped a few metres away, waiting for Maratse to examine Shellenberger.

"They could have sent a more talkative cop," she whispered, as I joined her. "This one's a moody bugger."

I stifled a laugh, and said, "You have no idea."

Maratse crouched by Shellenberger's body, looked to both sides and then rolled it over.

"Aren't you going to photograph the scene?" Arika asked as Maratse went through Shellenberger's pockets.

"Are these your footprints?" he said, pointing at the snow.

"Yes."

"And those?" Maratse pointed behind him.

"Yeah, they're mine."

"Did you kill him?"

"No." Arika started to say more but stopped when Maratse shrugged.

"You can move the body," he said. Maratse picked up Shellenberger's wallet and a small leather notebook that he had pulled out of the cargo pocket in the dead man's jacket. It looked like a diary. It looked old. Maratse walked back up the slope and handed it to me. "Your English is better than mine," he said.

"Is that it?" Arika said. "What about cause of death?"

Maratse shrugged. "The doctor will need to determine that."

"But what happens now? Do we just carry him onto the chopper and..." Arika reached out to tug at Maratse's jacket as he turned away. "Hey. Where are you going?"

Maratse waited for the two geologists to lift Shellenberger's body, and then crouched once again in the snow. He dipped his head, staring at the hollow beneath the curl of smooth glacier ice that turned north. He dropped to his knees, and then scraped at the snow with his hands.

"What have you found?" Arika said, as she jogged down to where Maratse lay flat in the ice.

"A tunnel," he said, as he wormed his way inside.

Part 2

Maratse crawled deeper into the snow tunnel until the only thing I could see of him was his boots. He would have gone further and beneath the tongue of ice if Arika hadn't grabbed his ankles and pulled, until he squirmed out of the hole to glare at her.

"There's someone inside," he said, brushing the snow from the front of his jacket. "Who else is missing?"

"A Greenlandic woman," Arika said. "I don't remember her name." She grabbed Maratse's sleeve as he ducked towards the tunnel entrance. "But I can't let you crawl in there. It's not safe." Arika pulled at Maratse's arm until he brushed her away. "You have no idea if the floor is ten metres or ten millimetres thick. You could be crawling into a crevasse. Let my team dig into the tunnel. We'll make sure it's safe. Then you can explore, if you really think someone is inside."

"*Iiji*," Maratse said. "Someone *is* inside."

I believed him. I had seen that look far too often to doubt him. But a crease of impatience played across Maratse's face as Arika explained her position on the team, and her responsibilities. It had nothing to do with her being a woman in charge. Maratse just didn't like waiting. But I wasn't sure that Arika understood that.

"You're questioning my authority?" she said, at

another crease across Maratse's brow. "If you are, then I suggest you go back to the camp, talk with Lærke – the expedition leader. She can show you the papers. If that doesn't satisfy you, you can call the government of Greenland, or the Danes, whoever you want. I don't care." Arika jabbed a finger at the entrance to the tunnel. "But no-one goes inside that tunnel until I've made it safe. Is that understood?"

Arika's face bloomed with a deep heat – I could feel the energy charging out of her body. But she didn't waver from her position. I wondered at her jurisdiction, and the point at which Maratse's jurisdiction would trump Arika's, but the thought was brushed aside as Arika called the camp on her radio and set her team in motion. Everyone else was to be confined inside the camp perimeter, until she said otherwise.

"Including you, Constable," she said, as she lowered her radio.

Maratse took one last look at the tunnel entrance, and then started walking back to the camp. "Hurry," he said, as he passed Arika.

I walked beside Maratse all the way. He said nothing more, but twice he paused to look back at the tunnel, and a third time when Arika's team rushed past. The shovels they carried reflected the spring sunlight and the ropes they wore slung over one shoulder bounced at their hips. Maratse watched them for a few seconds more, and then continued into camp.

One of the pilots from the helicopter waved to Maratse as we walked inside the camp perimeter.

He tapped his watch and said something about *flying hours*, before promising to return should Maratse need the helicopter.

"We'll take the body to the morgue at Thule Air Base. The doctor can look at him, but we'll keep him on ice until you get back. I guess he'll have to be repatriated as soon as the investigation is over."

"There's another person missing," Maratse said, tapping a cigarette out of the packet and into his hand. "We might need to coordinate a search."

"It looks like you've got plenty of people here already," the pilot said. "But keep us posted."

Maratse nodded, lit his cigarette and rolled it into the gap between his teeth. He stuffed his hands into his pockets as the pilot walked away. I followed him to the main tent, drawn by the chatter of the diesel generator, briefly masked by the helicopter's departure. I stood quietly and froze slowly, as Maratse finished his cigarette, breathing a silent sigh of relief when he opened the canvas fly of the tent and nodded for me to go inside. Maratse followed a second later.

The inside of the communal tent was arranged with four long tables with low benches on either side. I sat at the table closest to the gas heater, like the ones I had seen in the outdoor seating areas of Copenhagen cafés in autumn and early spring. Maratse spoke with Lærke, drawing her away from the computer to give her an update on the situation, and to glean more information from her about Josh Shellenberger and the missing Greenlander. I listened with half an ear and then remembered the diary Maratse had given me. I peeled off my gloves and tugged the diary out of my jacket pocket, removed the thick rubber bands that kept it closed, and then put it on the table.

The cover of the diary opened flat, as if it had been read many times. The pages were lined with a faint blue ink that stretched across each of the creamy yellow sheets of paper. The pages were yellow at the edges. Several of them had greasy stains that showed the writing from the other side. I closed the diary, ran my fingers over the thick cover, then opened it to the first page, searching for a name. I smiled when I saw it, and again when I found the date of the first entry. I looked up as Maratse's shadow fell on the table. He sat down and nodded at the diary.

"Is it Shellenberger's?"

"Yes," I said, "but I don't think it was Josh Shellenberger's diary. It might have been his father's. Look at this name." I pressed my finger to a name printed in tight capitals in the middle of the first page. "Frank Shellenberger," I said. "And the first entry is from May 2nd, 1960."

"Hmm." Maratse frowned as I turned the diary for him to see. "1960?"

"From what Josh told us the other night, the American Engineers – from the army – finished building Camp Century in 1960." I pulled the diary back across the table and flicked through the first few pages. "Josh said that army servicemen rotated back to America after 180 days. If Frank was here in 1960, it could be that he was one of the first men to actually serve inside the finished base."

"In 1960?"

"Yes," I said.

I opened the diary to the first page and started to read. Maratse stopped me. He pointed at the coffee urn on one of the far tables.

"I get the coffee, you read," he said. "Aloud."

"You want me to translate?"

"*Eeqqi*," he said, as he walked to the coffee urn. "Just read slowly."

I ran my fingers along the first few lines of Frank's diary, getting a feel for his handwriting. When Maratse returned with the coffee I was ready.

"I'll just start then," I said.

Maratse nodded.

"Okay then." I plunged into the first entry, catching up just as Frank did, after what he described as a hectic start *with a heck of a rush.*

May 2nd 1960

I'm still gettin' used to the light – all the time. So bright. But there's no time to get used to anythin'. Yesterday, and the day before that, was all about gettin' the "heavy swing" ready. The swing is a tractor train that leaves Tuto (Thule Take-off) headin' for Camp Century – the city beneath the ice. A heavy swing has the most tractors – they look like an amphibious tank on caterpillar tracks – and each tractor pulls a trailer carryin' a wannigan. The wannigans are wooden boxes – some of them have bunks, others are offices, then there's the science laboratories – those guys have got a few bunks stuffed inside of them, too. But Captain Walker told me two days ago – or was it three? It's so hard to keep track, what with there bein' no

*night 'n' all, but, anyways, Captain Walker said I
was drivin' one of the tractors. I was going to be a
"cat skinner". I figured I would be, but he's given
me the last in the swing – says I have to be on my
guard. What he actually said, word for word, was:
"It's a big responsibility, Frank. I think you can get
the job done. What about you? Do you think you
can do it, Frank?" Naturally, I told him "Yes, sir!"
and he shook my hand and told me to carry on.
Everyone round here likes the Captain, they even
call him Eugene when they're off duty, and
sometimes he hears them, and he acts like it's
alright, "but not too often, boys". That's what he
says. "Not too often."*

"He sounds young," Maratse said, as I paused
for a sip of coffee.

"I think he is. Straight out of training, and then
sent to Greenland – off on an adventure." The
writing was infectious, and I grinned at the thought
of a young man arriving at what must have been
strangest place he had ever seen. Maratse tapped the
diary, and I continued, skipping a few pages of
details about camp life until Frank's handwriting
changed, as if he was writing in a hurry, or with
great excitement. As I started to read, I realised it
was the latter.

*I was just gettin' settled in the seat of my cab when I
saw her again. The Eskimo girl. The boys say she's
from the camp down by the harbour, that she's lived
here all her life. They say she's about seventeen,
and gosh, she sure is pretty. It's the eyes – dark*

17

brown, but alive, like traffic lights – no, that's not right, but I don't know what to call them, or how to call them. Just that they're bright, flashin', and if she catches you – with those eyes, well, it's like lightnin'. I've been struck a few times already, includin' that first day I got off the ship. She was waitin' on the dock, gettin' in the way, but no-one told her to move. She just sat on one of those huge wooden crates of equipment, kickin' her heels against the side, wearin' those sealskin boots over a pair of cotton pants. She had a t-shirt on – nothin' more than that, and there was ice on the water, snow on the ground, and she's just sittin' there, as if it was the height of summer, if you please. Well, I noticed her – all the boys noticed her, what with all that black hair curlin' in the wind, and her smile. Then she comes by, wanderin' past the swing, and I'm in my tractor and she waves – at me. Not the others. (Well, she might have waved at them, but I don't care – she looked in my cab and waved at me!) Eugene – Captain Walker – he said we was to treat her nice, but to ignore her. "Don't encourage her," he said. But all I did was wave, and then watch her, from the cab. I heard one of the old timers say she wasn't wearin' a bra, that they probably didn't have bras in the Eskimo village. Well, I looked, and he was right.

"I think Frank is falling in love," I said.

"*Iiji.*" Maratse looked at his watch and then stood up. "I want to see how far they've got."

"Okay," I said. I started to close the book but stopped when I saw the next few lines. I lifted my hand, gesturing for Maratse to wait. "Just a little more," I said.

Once we got the heavy swing into motion, I forgot all about the girl. I had to concentrate all of a sudden. Drivin' those big cats on the ice, keepin' a good distance from the next tractor – not too far, not too close – it tuckers you out, I'll say. Then when we called it quits for the night, after just five miles, I was the first inside the wannigan. I found my bunk and I was just pullin' off my woollens, about ready to strip down, and then I heard it – I heard a giggle. That girl took a whole year off my life when she slid out from under the bunk. Then she hit me with that smile, and those eyes. Well, I forgot all about what Eugene said. I couldn't ignore her. She was right there. So, I put my hand on my chest and I said, "I'm Frank." I pointed at her and asked her what her name was. She looked on me like no girl has ever looked on me before, and she said, "Nialiánnguak." It took some time for me to say it, then longer to spell it. But that's who she is, and now I have to figure out how to tell the Captain. He's not going to be best pleased, but I don't think he'll turn us around. And that's alright by me.

Part 3

"Before you go," Lærke said, as Maratse walked towards the door. "I've got the information you wanted." Lærke waved Maratse over to her desk, and then stood up so that he could take her seat at the computer. "That's his application," she said, reaching around Maratse to open Josh Shellenberger's details on the screen. "I couldn't find much about the woman, other than her name." Lærke tapped the screen in the section reserved for *comments*. "I think you'll be able to say her name better than I can, Constable."

"Serminnguaq Satorana," he said. "She's from Qaanaaq, or maybe Savissivik."

"You know her?"

"I know her surname."

"There's not much more about her," Lærke said. "But as she required no transportation, and would meet us here, I didn't think much more about it. We've all been busy," she said. "It took some time to get the expedition approved. The government – all of them – seems to get concerned whenever an independent expedition wants to visit this area." She tapped the radiation badge on her jacket. "This probably has something to do with it."

"Hmm," Maratse said. He scrolled to the top of Shellenberger's application and pressed his nose close to the screen to read the text. He nodded and leaned back when Lærke suggested he enlarge the document. "*Qujanaq*," he said, settling back in the chair.

I leaned over Maratse's shoulder, quietly translating words when he pointed at them. According to his resume, Shellenberger was an accomplished historian with several publications to his credit, a host of articles in leading historical journals. He had one particular area of interest that formed the basis of his application to join the expedition, and that was the building and operation of Camp Century. A personal note confirmed what we had already gleaned from the diary, that Shellenberger's father had been stationed at Camp Century in the early years of its operation, before it was decommissioned.

"We're mostly concerned with ice," Lærke said, when Maratse nodded that he was finished. "It's unusual for a geology expedition to have any members other than scientists, students, and climbers. You've met Arika Jones," she said, with a quick glance at Maratse.

"*Iiji.*"

"She was against adding Shellenberger to the team, but I convinced her that his name would give us access to additional funds."

"And did it?" I asked.

"Oh yes," she said, gesturing at the inside of the tent and the gas heater. "We're not used to such luxury."

I was tempted to ask if Arika had approved my place on the team, but Maratse brought the conversation back to Shellenberger and his companion.

"What about Serminnguaq?"

"I remember meeting her, but she hardly said more than a few words. I'm not sure anyone spoke to her, actually."

"Where did she sleep?"

"She shared a tent with Josh."

"What was their relationship?"

"I couldn't say." Lærke looked away, as if she was remembering something. "They didn't seem close, but there was definitely something going on. The few times I saw them together, it always looked like they had just had an argument. But they held hands, more often than not."

"Shellenberger was fifty-three," Maratse said. "What about Serminnguaq?"

"I don't know," Lærke said. She lowered her eyes, and then said, "I'm sorry, I'm not good at guessing the age of Greenlanders'."

Maratse shrugged. "Neither am I." He pointed at the computer, and said, "Can you send me a copy of this?"

"Yes, of course."

Maratse tugged a grubby business card from his wallet and handed it to Lærke. "The email is on the back."

"And what are you going to do now?"

"Find Serminnguaq," Maratse said, as he stood up.

I stuffed the diary into my jacket pocket, pulled my gloves on and followed Maratse out of the tent. He smoked as we walked back to the tunnel, stopping on a rise just beyond the camp perimeter to look down at Arika and her team digging below. They had been busy since we left them, slotting aluminium slats into the grooves of metal posts screwed into the ice, shoring up the sides of the tunnel as they dug deeper under the ice.

"If anyone was in there," I said. "They would have found them by now. Don't you think?"

Maratse said nothing until he had finished his cigarette. He nodded at Arika's team, and said, "She won't come out until they are gone."

"You mean Serminnguaq?"

"*Iiji*." Maratse stuck his hands in his pockets. "We should wait. Tell me about Frank."

"You mean read some more of his diary?"

Maratse nodded, and I tugged the diary out of my pocket. The rubber bands were tricky to remove with gloves; Maratse did it for me. He held the diary for a moment, turning it in his hands, before handing it to me to read. I started with the entry for the following day.

May 3rd 1960
Captain Walker was mad alright, and the drivers, too. He made us all sleep in the one wannigan. It was warm but cramped like a doghouse. It smelled like one too. Nialiánnguak was supposed to sleep in the crew's wannigan all by herself, but she snuck into ours late in the night. If anyone heard her, they didn't say a word. I just kept real quiet, but I didn't sleep a wink, I could feel her body pressing against my toes. I couldn't say if it was her back or her belly, and I don't rightly know if I should even guess, but I knew she was there the whole night,

right up until the first driver woke, and she snuck out, hightailin' it back to her wannigan before anyone saw her. Captain Walker called a meeting over breakfast. He said we'd come too far to turn around, what with the weather 'n' all. And, he said, it wasn't safe to send one tractor back to base, even if he wanted to. He said he would call a helicopter to come and pick her up. But then one of the old timers said that wouldn't work, because they were strugglin' to adapt them to the cold. The new helicopters – the H34s – needed to be polar-oiled, and they hadn't done that since unloadin' them from the ships. It would be one, maybe two days before they were flyin' – weather dependin'. Two days! Weather dependin'. I hoped the Captain couldn't read minds, because I was giddy over the thought of that little Eskimo girl warmin' my feet for one or maybe two nights. I had no other intentions – cross my heart and tell my mother – but she was about the prettiest girl I ever seen, and I didn't mind that she stowed away on the heavy swing. I didn't put her there, I didn't ask her, but I didn't want to send her away either. Of course, the Captain can't read minds, but he can read faces. He said "Shellenberger," not Frank, so I knew I was in trouble. He said, "She's your responsibility. She rides in your cab. You keep her safe. And no screwing around." The men laughed at that, and I don't know whose face was redder – mine or the Captain's. He didn't mean anythin' by it, but the men laughed all the same. Some of them even complained that it wasn't fair, or that it wasn't smart to put her in my charge, but I was determined to do my best, and I told them so. One man laughed so hard at that, I stuck my face in his and, I declare, I would have hit him so, if the Captain hadn't intervened. He sent us back to our tractors, and he sent Nialiánnguak back to mine. I was still fumin' over that lard ass with the smart comment, but I wouldn't show it. I opened the door for Nialiánnguak, and I found her a big jacket. She disappeared right inside it, and I laughed. She laughed too – the sweetest sound I ever heard. Then I started the tractor – all the tractors started – and the heavy swing swung into motion. She chatted the whole time, and I didn't understand a word. But my jaw ached from smilin', all the way until the next stop, and then some.

I closed the diary, snapped the rubber bands around it, and tucked it away. I had a good idea where the story was headed, and I questioned Captain Walker's reasoning behind putting young Frank Shellenberger in charge of Nialiánnguak. But maybe he didn't have a better alternative? I couldn't find a reference to Frank's age, but I guessed he was in his early twenties. Stuck in a tractor cabin with a pretty *Eskimo girl*. Frank's diary had all the ingredients for a romantic novel, but the next instalment would have to wait, as Maratse walked down towards the tunnel.

Arika met us at the entrance. Her jacket hung from a ski pole, and heat steamed from her body. She shook her head and pressed her palm into Maratse's chest as he tried to walk around her.

"We've only just begun."

"You've dug the entrance," Maratse said.

"We've widened it and made it safe."

"And you've found the way in?"

"Sure, but you have to understand, if this is part of one of Camp Century's tunnels, it's been twisted and deformed for fifty years, moving down the ice cap towards the sea. It's just pure luck that there's a hole in there at all. My guess is, from what we've seen, it must have been one of the larger halls that's been compressed into something like a tunnel. We found splinters and the odd plank of wood, probably from a building they left inside. But it's not a tunnel, not like you think it is, anyway."

"But there is a space inside," Maratse said. It wasn't a question.

"Yes," Arika said. "But no-one's going in there, until it's safe." The snow crunched beneath Arika's boots as she shuffled back a step. "Look," she said, with a softer inflection in her voice. "If anyone's hiding inside there, they're too scared to come out right now, what with us working right outside. There's a gap, so there's air." She paused to look up at the sky. "I don't like the looks of those clouds, but we'll keep going until we have to stop. I can send someone for you as soon as we're done. How about you wait back at camp?" She looked at Maratse and then turned to me. "I could use a weather report, and a fresh battery for the radio."

"I can get it," I said, pleased to have an excuse to go back to the tent. I had been cold in Greenland before, colder than this, but standing around on the ice chilled my bones. Maratse, as usual, seemed wholly unaffected.

"Do you have an extra shovel?" he asked.

"Yes," Arika said.

"Then I'd like to dig."

Maratse walked down to the tunnel entrance as Arika gave me her radio. She explained where the spare batteries were and said that Lærke would be able to provide the weather report.

"One more thing," she said, touching my arm as I turned to leave.

"Yes?"

"Do you know him? The Constable?"

"Yes," I said. "We've met several times."

"Is he always like this?"

I had an idea what she meant, but a simple *yes* or *no* never seemed adequate when describing Maratse. I could try and explain his passion for the land, and how that was only ever exceeded by his love for his people, but it was never something that he expressed, certainly not though emotions. Maratse showed his feelings through his actions. He struggled with waiting when waiting seemed counterproductive, and yet he never hurried, especially when the weather, the land, or the sea – more often than not, the ice – determined otherwise. But when people were in danger, Maratse's patience had a limit; it was just difficult to know when he had reached it. I settled for the easy answer.

"Yes," I said. "He's always like this."

Part 4

It took less than ten minutes to grab a new battery for Arika's radio. Lærke promised to give Arika a weather report as soon I took the radio back to her. I lingered for a second as Arika took the radio. Maratse's jacket hung on a ski pole next to hers and he dug alongside the young members of Arika's safety crew, swapping the occasional grunt, as was his way. I could have helped, and I'm ashamed to say I didn't, but I felt my time could be better spent finding out what happened to Frank and Nialiánnguak. I told Arika I would be in the main tent if she or Maratse needed me. I think she heard what I said, but it was lost in the storm warning filtering through the radio, intensified by the urgency in Lærke's voice. I shuffled across the ice, stepped into the camp perimeter, and then hurried to the main tent. I told myself that I was doing my bit to help find out what had happened to Josh Shellenberger, and guiltily helped myself to another mug of coffee. The tent was warmer than when I fetched the battery – more people. I found a spot on a bench furthest from the heater and started to read.

May 3rd 1960
The visibility got real bad after lunch. Captain Walker had warned us about a storm, and once the snow started we slowed to a crawl. Normally, a

heavy swing could get from Tuto to Camp Century in about 3-5 days, but a storm would mean double that, at least. We crawled to a stop, but Captain Walker told us to stay in our cabs, just in case it cleared. We kept the engines runnin' for heat. Then his voice crackled over the radio orderin' us to stay in our cabs, because he didn't want to lose anyone in the storm. I couldn't even see the hood of my own tractor, let alone the next tractor in the train. I was goin' nowhere. Now, Nialiánnguak started chatting, and I chatted right back. I think we both told different stories, with a pause to let the other nod or say somethin' as if we understood what the story was about. For my part, I tried to explain why they called the drivers "cat skinners", but they don't have cats in Greenland – leastways I had never seen one – and they don't have caterpillars neither. So when I mimed that I was skinnin' a cat, or bunched my finger like a hungry caterpillar, she just laughed, and darn near melted my heart. Of course, it got strange then. Not strange, but hot. I almost turned down the heat. Then she shrugged off that jacket, and then she pulled off her t-shirt, and the old timers were right – they don't have bras in Greenland. I couldn't take my eyes off of her. Even the thought of Captain Walker bangin' on the side of my tractor, or hollerin' for me to get out and roll in the snow to cool down... I had those thoughts, but they didn't last. Because then all I could think of was that pretty little Eskimo girl, how Captain Walker had ordered me to look after her, then ordered us to stay in our cabs, and then, well he didn't order anythin' else, but what else could I do?

I don't mind sayin' that I was not experienced in these kinds of things, and I don't mind admittin' that I was right afeared in the start, wonderin' if I would do things right, if I could do what she wanted. But Nialiánnguak knew what to do. She knew plenty. She helped me through the whole thing – helped me out of my clothes until we were both buck-naked, then helped me some more. I don't remember ever feelin' that way before, but of course, my heart – I remember it beatin' so loud, so fast, I remember strugglin' for breath. I must have been red-faced, so bad she slowed down. I remember rollin' down the window, just needin' some air. That felt better, and then we… well we did it then. I don't know as to what I can say. No more than that. It was better than I had heard – better even than I had dreamed. What with the storm n' all, it was probably better than anythin' I would ever do or feel again. I held her through that storm. I held her right close. Then, when we started to cool, well, I just tugged that old jacket on top of us, and we stayed there through the night until mornin'. The wind didn't let up. We stayed there the whole next day too. Plenty of food in a tractor – and plenty to do, now that the Captain ordered us to stay there.

I closed the diary, sipped my coffee, and then took a moment to look around the tent. The sides of the tent snapped, sometimes billowing when a big fist of wind punched against them. I hadn't noticed, and thought nothing more of it, until one of the geologists said something about me being an *old timer*, and I laughed at that.

"No," I said. "Just got stuck in my book."

"What book is that?"

I didn't have an answer for that. It seemed inappropriate to tell the other members of the expedition that I was reading the diary Maratse had found on the body of Josh Shellenberger. They mentioned him in between gusts, and I suddenly felt awkward.

It was Maratse who saved me, together with Arika and her safety crew as they blustered into the tent, snow swirling from their bodies in the wind, until the last member of the team stepped inside and secured the flap of the tent. Maratse grunted something about coffee and stalked towards the urn as soon as Arika unclipped him from the safety line she had attached to his utility belt.

"I told him we would start again, as soon as the wind dropped," Arika said, as she sat down at my table. "But he's convinced she's inside the tunnel, and that we're wasting time."

"We are," Maratse said, as he sat down next to her. He pushed a mug of coffee into her hands, and then sipped at his own.

"This wind," Arika said, "is coming right off the top of the ice cap. There's no way we can dig in this." She sighed as she warmed her hands around the mug. "The snow will blow into the tunnel. If this lasts for too long, we'll have to dig it all over again. You're sure she's inside?"

"*Iiji*," Maratse said, with a nod of his head.

"But how can you know that? For certain."

"I don't," he said. "But where else can she go?"

I waited for Arika to respond, and then, when

she didn't, I turned the diary towards Maratse and ran my finger along the last line on the page.

"Frank slept with Nialiánnguak," I said.

"Slept with?"

"Had *sex* with," I said. "They were stuck inside the cab of his tractor, in a storm. The whole night. So far, anyway."

"Who's Frank?" Arika asked.

"We think it's Shellenberger's father."

"That's the diary you found in Josh's pocket?"

"Yes. Maratse gave it to me to read."

"My English is a little rusty," Maratse said. "He helps."

Arika turned her head slightly, just enough to add a little more weight to the look she gave me. "It's weird," she said. "I'm getting this strange vibe that the two of you are like Holmes and Watson, or something, only not so smart." Arika laughed. "Sorry. You know what I mean."

I did, and I could see the similarity. But while Maratse was too quiet and too reserved to ever reveal just how smart he actually was, it was the setting that ruined any further similarities. The wind thumping against the sides of the tent. The twenty-four-hour sunlight tempered and filtered by the snow clouds, and the temperature, plummeting as the wind leached it out of our bodies, forcing Lærke and one of the expedition members to change the cylinder for the gas heater before the wind showed any signs of abating.

"What happened next?" Maratse asked, with a nod at the diary,

I turned the next page, pausing as the geologists

from the surrounding tables and the diggers from Arika's team crowded onto our benches, with more rearranging the tables behind us so that they could sit close, leaning in against the wind.

"This is Josh's father's diary. Frank Shellenberger – Josh's dad – has just spent the night in the cab of his tractor," I said, bringing them all up to speed. "He was on his way to Camp Century. He's a young man, and there's a young Greenlandic woman with him." One of the geologists made a gentle *ooh* sound, and we all paused, wondering if it was appropriate until Lærke cleared her throat and announced we were out of gas.

"So, huddle up," she said, with a nod to me. "If you're ready?"

I pressed my finger to the page, pitching my voice a little higher as I started to read.

May 4th 1960

It was foggy the next mornin' – a real pea souper. I had a fright when Captain Walker banged on the side of the tractor. Nialiánnguak was sleeping in my arms. I gave her a quick shove and sat bolt upright in my seat, just as the Captain climbed up onto the runnin' boards and opened the cab door. He sniffed at the air as he climbed in and I wondered if he guessed somethin'. I had thought about what I might say if he asked. In fact, I had thought about it all night. Nialiánnguak had snored – she even snored pretty – and I hadn't slept one bit. I thought about my heart too, and if I was to get that excited every time I was with a woman, then I might want to see a doctor about it, although just what I would say to him, I don't know. Anyway, Captain Walker said somethin' about the fog, but that we would keep driving. I said I didn't know as to how we would do that, and he just smiled and pointed at the roof. "I'm sending someone to your cab," he said. "This fog is a ground fog, just a few metres high. If you stand on the roof you can see the top of the wannigan in front of you. You'll drive and Smith will give you directions." He told me to repeat the instructions back to him, and then he got ready to leave. But before he went, he cast a quick look at Nialiánnguak. Her jacket was open, and the Captain and me could see the creamy brown skin of her belly, and a bit more besides. She didn't seem to care. She just smiled. Then I saw how her hair was wild and tangled, and I felt that grip on my heart again, and I got all red-faced. In fact, Captain Walker was so concerned he forgot all about Nialiánnguak. Or, at least I thought he did. On his way out of the cab, he picked up her t-shirt and tossed it into her lap. He muttered somethin' before he slipped out of the cab and dropped down to the ice. He left the door open, and I wonder if he did it on purpose, because when I leaned out to grab the handle and close it, he was right there by the door, lookin' up at me. I'll never forget what he said, and I'm not sure he meant to say it, but it made me laugh anyways. Captain Walker looked up at me, and he said, "Carry on, soldier."

"I get it now," said the young geologist who had asked me what I was reading. "It's better than the books I've got in my tent."

"It's real, too," said another geologist. She thumped the arm of the woman next to her. "Imagine being stuck inside a cab on the ice cap, with a bloke. Nothing to do. There's a storm blowing…"

They carried on, embellishing the story as they sat out the storm, emptying the coffee urn, making a new batch, sharing similar stories, then agreeing that nothing came close, until someone prompted Arika to tell the one about the dentist in the cable car.

I closed the diary and made myself comfortable, as Arika worked her face through a series of protestations, saying that she wasn't going to tell that story, and then, a second later, that she would, as soon as there was more coffee. Someone reached over the huddle of geologists and thrust a fresh mug into her hand. Arika cleared her throat, but I didn't hear a word of what she said, I was too busy watching Maratse as he quietly wormed his way through the expedition crowd and slipped out of the tent.

"Serminnguaq Satorana," he said, as I ducked under the tent flap and joined him outside. The wind whipped at the collar of my jacket and I cupped my hands over my ears, leaning close to Maratse as he continued. "The woman in the tunnel."

"Yes?"

"She's Frank Shellenberger's daughter."

Part 5

The wind cut through the folds of my jacket, penetrating the zip, stuffing cold air into the pockets of space under my arms, around my ribs, anywhere it pleased. Even Maratse dipped his bare head into the wind, and I followed him, one hand tucked into the back of his utility belt, as he led the way back to the tunnel. The wind had dumped fresh snow inside the trench dug by Arika and her team. We waded through it. The going was slightly easier, on account of the trench wall providing some, if not a lot, of protection from the wind. Two shovels marked the entrance to the tunnel. Maratse tugged one out of the snow and pressed it into my chest. He picked up the other one, pointed to his right, then dug to his left. I joined him, digging and scraping the snow clear of the entrance, cursing the wind as it swirled spindrifts of snow down my neck, or lifted the skirt of my jacket to stuff more snow up my back. I remember the first trickle of sweat being a welcome relief, a kind of rebellion against the cold wind. But Maratse warned me not to get too hot, placing his hand on my arm, and pulling me onto my knees, out of the wind.

"We can get inside now," he said, scraping snow to form a lip around the entrance. He slid the shovel inside the tunnel, and ducked, ready to follow it.

"You don't think we should wait?"

"Serminnguaq has waited long enough."

Maratse squirmed over the lip of snow and through the entrance. I watched his boots disappear, then followed him, only to return for the snow shovel the second Maratse noticed I had left it outside. When I returned, I was surprised to see that the sunlight filtered through to a certain depth in the ice, providing more light than I had expected. It was enough to see several metres further into the tunnel, to a point where it twisted sharply to the right. Maratse crawled on ahead of me and I followed.

It grew darker at the turn, but mercifully warmer, and quieter. The wind rasped and raged at the surface, but for all we could hear or feel of it, it might has well have been but a breeze, sinking to our knees as the air cooled inside the Greenland ice cap. I remembered something about climbers digging snow holes and pressing ski poles through the roofs, waggling them every now and again to keep a tube of air flowing into the snow hole. Even if we had ski poles, the ice was too thick, too deep and too strong to chip a breathing hole through it. I just hoped Serminnguaq had not gone too far. It crossed my mind that it would be hard work to drag a body through the tunnel. Perhaps that was what urged Maratse on. He crawled faster, until the ice floor curved away beneath us, opening like a huge tongue sticking out of a cheeky child's mouth. I bumped into Maratse, blinked in the gloom, and then gasped at the sight of wood timbers, some of them warped, others splintered, but arranged in a wall that might have been the side of a building erected inside the original Camp Century. It didn't seem likely, but there was no other explanation. I closed my fingers around the radiation badge fixed to my chest pocket and wondered if we were exposed to radioactive waste, and what that would mean, how it would affect us. Perhaps that was the story my editor wanted me to write? I think he suspected the climbers on the expedition to be secret activists, and Arika fit the profile perfectly – displaying a fierce dedication to her trade, and a deep respect for nature. But whatever the official or unofficial reason for the expedition, it was the human aspect that had brought Maratse to the ice cap, and *that* was the story I would write – to hell with my editor.

"There," Maratse said, pointing into the darkness.

I followed the direction of his finger, and then saw a dark shape curled on the ice. The ceiling was higher than in the first part of the tunnel, and I could sit with my chin on my chest. I did so as Maratse crawled towards the shape that I guessed was Serminnguaq. She had found a good hiding place, although I wondered how long she could stay down here without freezing or suffocating. I thought about hypothermia, struggling to remember if it was slurred speech, or shivering that came first. But there was nothing wrong with Serminnguaq's speech when Maratse reached her.

The hollow beneath the ice cap echoed with a sudden roar of hoarse Greenlandic; she flung a torrent of consonants and so very few vowels at the walls. I could hear the grief wrapped around each word even though I couldn't understand the words themselves. Maratse's voice was soft by comparison. I heard him repeat the same word again and again, variations of pitch, but always soft, until Serminnguaq's shouts became sobs, and each heave of her chest rocked her body closer to Maratse, until he had her in his arms, and he held her so tight, too tight to shout.

Even then, with my chin buried against my chest, and the cold seeping through the seat of my trousers, chilling my spine, I couldn't help but wonder at the change that came over Maratse each time he came in contact with his people. Old or young, it didn't matter. Maratse, the taciturn constable, wore his badge on his jacket but his heart on his sleeve. I tilted my head to watch as he held Serminnguaq, rocking with her as she sobbed, until her tears glistened, cooling in tiny streams on his jacket. Maratse beckoned for me to come closer as Serminnguaq started to talk.

Her first words were a confession of murder – at least, that's what Maratse told me, as he translated her Greenlandic into Danish.

"Make a note," he whispered, and I patted my pockets for a pencil, having already learned that pens were susceptible to the cold. But I had no notebook, and I said as much. "The diary," Maratse said.

"Of course," I said, nodding as I tugged it out of my pocket. It seemed fitting to record Serminnguaq's story in Frank Shellenberger's diary, especially if she was his daughter. I turned to the blank pages at the back, and made a note of the date, in the same style as Frank started each of his entries, and then I started writing, as Maratse translated.

I was born in January, in a hunter's cabin somewhere on the coast between Thule Air Base and Qaanaaq. My mother, Nialiánnguak, had been sick, but she had been travelling with her father – my ata – by sledge. No-one knew she was pregnant – she was slim, with a tiny belly, and the winter furs hid the rest. But when she started to complain of cramps, ata got scared. They were coming home, but he stopped at the cabin. Her waters broke on the snow. Ata carried her into the cabin. He lit a fire in the stove, then helped her out of her furs. I was born within an hour of them arriving at the sledge. The first light I saw was flame light, and the only warmth was my mother's skin, but that soon cooled as she died shortly after giving birth.

I was grateful when Maratse paused. The image of a lonely cabin beneath the black sky of winter, flame light licking at the wax paper windows, was strong, all the more so for hearing about it inside a tunnel wormed into the ice cap. I thought of Serminnguaq's first hours, and the grief her grandfather must have felt at losing his daughter. I imagined him carrying Nialiánnguak's body to the sledge, securing her to the wooden thwarts with cords of sealskin. How would he carry the baby? How would her keep her warm? Maratse explained as Serminnguaq continued.

Ata carried me inside his furs, pressed against his bare chest. He told me this every January of my childhood, how he tied a length of cord around his waist, pinching the sealskin smock to his body. He said he had to breathe through his mouth, exhaling to one side, for fear of his breath freezing on my face. He sledged back to Qaanaaq – it was closer – and he found a cousin to look after me, while he searched for a place to bury my mother. The ground was too hard to dig – frozen. They made a coffin, and my mother lay in it through the winter, on top of a low roof, until they buried her in mid-July. I stayed in Qaanaaq, growing up alongside my second cousins, greeting my ata every spring when he travelled across the ice from Thule. When I was six years old, I went with him, back to Thule. He took me up to the Americans. He told them that one of their soldiers was my father. They turned him away, said he had no proof. But he pointed at my fair skin and told them to find a Greenlander with white skin like his granddaughter's. When they ignored him, he got angry, and they escorted him back to the village looking out on to what they called North Star Bay, in the shadow of Mount Dundas. And that was where I lived then, because ata got sick, and he died late that same summer. I was six years old. I never knew my grandmother, but a friend of hers took me in, and I lived with them until they sent me to school in Upernavik. I didn't go back to Thule for many years. But when I did go back – I was twenty years old – the woman who had cared for me said a man had come looking for me, that he had left something for me.

Maratse stopped translating as Serminnguaq pushed at his arms and pointed at the diary in my hands. She switched to Danish, and said, "The man left me a letter, but I couldn't read it."

"Was that man Josh Shellenberger?" I asked.

"*Aap*," she said. "He came all the way from America to find me. He carried that diary with him."

"Did you read it?"

"I can't read it. I can't read English. But it doesn't matter anymore. He is dead. I killed him."

I wasn't ready for the shriek that followed as Serminnguaq's character altered as if she had flipped a switch. She railed against Maratse's chest with her fists, forcing him backwards, before she turned on her knees, revealing a small, dark hole in the ice behind her. She slid inside it, kicking at Maratse's hands as he clutched her ankles. She kicked free and slid out of sight. Maratse lurched after her, and he would have followed if I hadn't grabbed him by the shoulder, dropping the diary onto the ice beside me, as I pulled him away from the hole.

"You don't know where it goes," I said. "You don't know if you will be able to get out."

"That doesn't matter," he said.

"Yes," I said. "Yes, it does. It matters, Constable, because you don't have to die to save her. That's not how this works."

"You don't know how this *works*," he said.

"No, but Arika, back at the camp – she knows *ice*. You know *people*. If you work together, you

42

can still save her, without getting trapped beneath the ice."

For a moment I thought he was going to shrug free of my hand and plunge into the darkness after Serminnguaq, but he settled, relaxing his shoulders as he leaned his back against the tunnel's icy wall.

"She is ashamed," he said. "She feels guilty. She thinks she killed Shellenberger."

"But you don't think so?"

"*Eeqqi*," Maratse said, with a shake of his head. He looked at the diary, pointing as I picked it up. "The answer's in there. I will go for help. You keep reading."

Part 6

May 4th 1960

Smith crawled onto the roof just as Captain Walker said he would, and he steered us in the tracks of the tractor in front of us. We kept goin' for eight hours, stoppin' twice to refuel, before Captain Walker called it a night. All the men bunked down in the wannigan to give Nialiánnguak some privacy. She didn't like it all that much, but Captain Walker gave up his own bunk in the officers' wannigan to sleep by the door of ours. When Nialiánnguak sneaked over to our wannigan early the next mornin', she got such a fright, she woke us all up with her screamin'. It might have been funny, but all I could think of was her, the smell of her skin, the tickle of her hair. But after he sent her packin', back to the her own wannigan, Captain Walker looked on me, and said, "Carry on, soldier." He even tried to put her in another cab, with another driver the next mornin', but she put up such a fight, he had to let her ride with me, if we were ever goin' to keep to the schedule.

I dropped the diary into my lap and breathed on my fingers. My breath frosted between the fibres of my gloves, and I started to wonder if Maratse was coming back. I didn't believe it could ever happen, but what if he lost his way? What if he got disorientated in the storm? I might have died in that tunnel, too tired and too cold to get myself out. I leaned over the hole in the ice and looked down into the cavity below. The surface was black and knobbly, with less light filtering through, a dark place full of shadows. I couldn't see Serminnguaq, and I didn't want to call out for fear of forcing her deeper into the cave. At least, I thought it was a cave. From the little I could see, it brought to mind pictures I had seen in magazines of caves beneath glaciers, with rocky floors and ice ceilings, pitted with lumps of granite and other debris like a cookie dough, kept in the freezer, away from greedy fingers. Of course, now you could buy frozen cookie dough ice cream, so the analogy wasn't a good one, but it did distract me for a moment, so much so I didn't hear Arika crawling through the tunnel until she called out.

"Is that the hole?" she asked, tugging a loose strand of her hair caught in the clip of her helmet strap.

"What?" I spun around, almost guilty at the thought of being caught out, but not knowing why. "Yes," I said. "She's down there."

Arika crawled to where I sat hunched over the diary. She squeezed past me and I gave her some room to look down into the cave below. She unclipped the head torch from her helmet, leaned inside the hole, and shone it around inside. She called out to Serminnguaq but got no reply.

"We'll have to rope up before going in there," she said.

"Yes," I said, hoping she didn't mean me.

Arika crawled away from the hole and rested for a moment. She gave me a look that reeked of trouble, and I knew *I* was the one who had broken one of her laws, never mind that I was with a police officer when I did it. I was still waiting for Maratse's jurisdiction to kick in, but until then I decided to save my own skin.

"I told the Constable he would need your help," I said.

Arika dipped her head as she clipped the head torch back onto her helmet. When she looked up, I got the full treatment – the harsh tones *and* the accusatory spotlight.

"And so you should have," she said. "But now you need to get out so we can open up that hole and rope in."

I closed the diary, tucked it into my pocket along with the pencil, and crawled towards Arika. She showed no intention of moving when I reached her position, choosing to make things difficult instead.

"I agreed to you being on this expedition, because I thought you might be useful," she said.

"In what way?"

"To send a message. Your magazine – *The Narwhal* – has a pretty large readership. If you did a piece on the radioactive waste in this area, and how it's been ignored all these years, I might be tempted to put in a good word with Lærke, and let you stay on."

"And if I don't?"

"You've disobeyed my orders a couple of times now…"

I couldn't remember the second time, but let it pass as Arika moved to one side.

"...I could easily put you on the chopper when it comes to pick up Maratse."

"And Serminnguaq," I said. "I suppose she will be leaving too."

"If we can get her out. Yes, of course."

I nodded, then crawled past Arika and into the first section of the tunnel. I heard the metallic clack of karabiners and other climbing equipment being organised just outside the entrance. Maratse took my hand when I reached it, pulling me out into a whole new world, with brilliant sunshine and little more than a lick of wind to remind one were in the Arctic.

"They're going to bring her out," Maratse said. "I promised to stay here."

He tapped a cigarette out of the packet and stuck it between his lips. Maratse flicked the lighter, only to pause as one of Arika's team told him to stop.

"You don't smoke near climbing ropes," he said. "The ash can melt a spot, and you'll never know. It'll be weak then, and that day you're climbing, and it snags, that weak spot will be the death of you. Just like smoking."

I caught the look on Maratse's face and stifled a laugh. The young man could have just asked him not to smoke. Maybe he needed to explain things, taking control of at least one thing in a strange environment. It probably gave him a measure of confidence that had been shaken by the historian's death, followed by the storm. Maratse shrugged, climbed out of the trench, and chose a spot to smoke a suitable distance from the climbers as they arranged their gear. I dug the toes of my boots into the same snow steps cut into the wall of the trench and climbed up to join him.

"Serminnguaq thinks she killed Shellenberger," Maratse said. "If we're going to get her to come out of the cave, I need to tell her she didn't."

"Yes," I said.

"So, you need to read."

I opened my jacket pocket and took out the diary. The light wind curled the edges and cooled the tips of my fingers, but not enough to stop me reading.

May 5th 1960

The weather was pretty good today, but I wasn't. If it hadn't been for Nialiánnguak, I might have had it even worse. It happened in the second hour. We were drivin' at a good pace, careful, but no stops. The wind was strong, and it was playin' hell with the radios. There was some snow blowin' between the tractors, makin' it difficult to see out of the mirrors, though it was easy enough to see the tractor in front. But we were at the back. I had another attack, where I just felt like everythin' was pumpin', blood rushin' to my head, in my temples. I felt like my face would be red, if I could look at it, but I didn't want to look at it. I carried on for a bit, but then I just felt I had to stop. I took my foot off the gas, and then I just slumped over the wheel. Nialiánnguak was hollerin' but I didn't understand what she said, and I didn't much care – I felt that bad. I remember lookin' ahead, thinkin' that the tractor in front was pullin' away. I wondered why he didn't stop. But he kept gettin' further and further – at least 300 metres. That's when Nialiánnguak opened the door and jumped out of the cab, down onto the ice. She ran after the tractor, her hair blowin' sideways in the wind. That was the last I remember seein' of her – that big old jacket flappin' like a cape behind her, hair twistin', arms wavin'. When the tractor stopped, she turned and I saw her face, those big brown eyes. Even in the state I was, it was like I was lookin' through a telescope or some such. She looked so pretty, even though she looked so scared. In that moment, when I thought I might even die, I just thanked God that I had met her, so pretty, so wild, so free and innocent. She belonged on the ice and she belonged everywhere, and if I could, I would have bought her a penthouse, draped her in diamonds, showered her in affection. But she just stood there, on the ice, pointin' and screamin' until Captain Walker and a few of the men came runnin' past her. And that was all I remembered. They told me they called in one of the helicopters. And they told me she flew back to the base with me. But I don't remember. I only remember wakin' up in America. In a hospital bed, with the doctor tellin' me he had operated on my heart, that I had a congenital defect. But I don't know about that. My body was in America, but my heart was back on the icecap.

It didn't require much imagination for me to picture Nialiánnguak waving her arms on the icecap. She could have been right behind us, calling to us. I wondered if Maratse thought the same thing. But, of course, we both knew that Nialiánnguak wouldn't live longer than the period of her pregnancy before she died in a remote hunters' cabin, under a cold black sky. I wondered if Frank ever knew and what he would have done if he had?

"Is there more?" Maratse asked.

I flipped through one blank page after another, shaking my head until I came to the middle of the book. There was a thin envelope tucked between the pages. I opened it, carefully, pausing at a new pillow of wind blowing up from the surface of the ice. I tucked my fingers into the envelope when it passed and pulled out a newspaper clipping – a thin column, folded in the middle.

"A wedding announcement," I said, peering at the tiny print. "Frank was married in 1961." There was another piece of paper inside the envelope, but a stronger gust of wind made pinch the envelope, stuffing it back inside the diary to protect it. I stuffed the diary back into my pocket.

"Hmm," Maratse said. He lit another cigarette.

"I suppose he never did come back for Nialiánnguak."

"They rarely do."

"What's that?"

Maratse plucked his cigarette from his lips and snubbed it out. He stuffed it back into the packet and tucked it away in the breast pocket of his jacket. He took a long breath and then sighed, kicking idly at the ice beneath his feet with the toe of his boot.

"This area," he said, with a curt nod that

seemed to encompass far more than we could see, "has had a lot of visitors over the years. Explorers, geologists, traders. A lot of people. Mostly men, coming and going after a short time, especially back then."

"You mean the '60s?"

"And before." Maratse pointed in the direction of Qaanaaq, far to the north. "You can still see it in the settlements and tiny villages along the coast. History says Greenlanders needed new blood to keep the community healthy. You can believe that if you want, just like you can believe the visitors were more than happy to oblige."

I wasn't used to Maratse saying so much at one time, And so, despite the cold in my fingers and my feet, I kept still and silent.

"Anyone reading that diary," he said, "will think Nialiánnguak was a quick woman."

"*Fast*," I said, suppressing the little smile that crept onto my lips. If Maratse saw it, he didn't react.

"But they never think about life up here. You need to live life, every day, because you don't know when it's going to end. You can wait for tomorrow, but tomorrow might end with an iceberg calving, or the ice breaking, or..." Maratse shrugged. "You have to live for today," he said. "Nialiánnguak lived for today."

He kicked once more at the ice, and then walked back towards the tunnel. I watched him for a moment, thinking about what he just said, thinking about Nialiánnguak, and Serminnguaq.

"Constable?" I said, jogging after him. "Arika

said she'd call us when they were ready."

"Hmm," he said. "I know, but I'm not going to wait."

Part 7

There were metal ice screws along the right-hand side of the tunnel, through the hole into the low-ceilinged chamber and all the way to the cave entrance. One of Arika's young climbers worked his way along the tunnel to the exit, clipping a rope into the screws to make a handrail. It seemed excessive, but it looked safe. He crawled out of the tunnel and stood in front of it.

"Arika says you have to wear a helmet," he said, pointing at two helmets and harnesses hanging from ice axes jammed into the side of the trench. Maratse grunted and picked up a helmet. "Not so fast, she said you need to wear a harness too." The climber pointed at Maratse's utility belt, then gestured at the pistol holstered above Maratse's right hip. "You can't wear both," he said.

"*Eeqqi*," Maratse said. "I guess I can't." He stuck the helmet onto his head and pushed past the climber, ignoring his protests as he ducked inside the tunnel.

I grabbed a helmet and the two harnesses, promising to make Maratse wear one of them, "Just as soon as I catch up with him." I followed Maratse inside the tunnel, and all the way to where Arika and one of her team waited at the entrance to the cave.

"I can get you down there," she said, "but

you'll need a harness."

Maratse nodded. He unbuckled his utility belt and pushed it to one side. Arika watched as I gave Maratse a climbing harness and he twisted into it.

"It's easier to rope in if you're wearing gloves." She tugged a fancy pair of leather gloves off her hands and pressed them into Maratse's. "You can wear mine."

"*Qujanaq*," he said, before clipping into the metal figure eight rappelling device Arika had prepared.

"You've done this before?"

"Once," Maratse said. "At the Academy."

"Okay," Arika said. "Hold the rope that comes out of the figure eight tight against your thigh. Lift your hand and let the rope slide through your fingers when you want to go down. Hold it tight when you want to stop. Got it?"

Maratse peered into the cave for a moment before looking at Arika. "Serminnguaq just crawled in."

"Yes, she did, but I want *you* to use a rope."

"Okay," he said. Maratse looked at me as he turned around to crawl backwards into the cave. "You're sure there's nothing more in the diary?"

"I'll look," I said, remembering the envelope.

Maratse nodded once more, then disappeared into the cave.

"Wait," Arika said. She pulled a head lamp out of her pocket, reached into the cave, and clipped it to the front of Maratse's helmet. "Shout when you need us."

The light from Maratse's head lamp flickered

around the ice walls as he descended, while I opened the diary and pulled out the envelope. I let the diary sit open in my lap and placed the marriage clipping between the pages. The second piece of paper was larger and tucked inside the envelope. The fit was so tight it seemed natural to think they were original, that they were a pair. I opened the letter and turned it within the light from Arika's head lamp.

"What is it?"

"A letter from the doctor," I said.

"What about?"

"Confirming something."

It seemed that doctors of all countries shared the same need to explain things in medical terms, when layman's terms would have been far simpler. I remembered friends telling me about their conditions, only to have to find a word that I would understand in the very next sentence. I was guilty of it too, telling *my* friends I had *influenza* when I could have just told them I had a cold. There was something more dramatic and more important about a medical term, and something more sinister too.

I looked up at a shout from Maratse, that he had reached the bottom of the cave, followed by another, when he called out to say he had found Serminnguaq.

"I'm sending a harness down to you," Arika said, clipping a spare harness around the rope. "Coming now." The karabiner hummed along the rope until it clunked against Maratse's harness at the bottom.

I tapped Arika on the shoulder and asked for

more light.

"It's a letter about the Schellenbergers' son," I said.

"Josh's parents?"

"Yes. Frank and a woman called Mary Jane. He must have married shortly after he got home from Greenland. They had one son," I said, turning the letter in the light. "His name was Joshua, and he had a congenital heart defect – a failure in the structure of the heart, basically a birth defect."

"So, Josh died from heart failure?"

"It seems likely," I said. "Hereditary. It says as much in his father's diary."

The letter fell into shadow, as Arika looked down into the cave. "Then why did Serminnguaq run?"

Given the time I had spent in Greenland already, I thought I had the answer. Through the many experiences I had shared with Maratse, I had learned something about shame. I understood it to be a simple emotion, a driving factor that influenced many of the terrible events that had played out in the mountains and on the ice of Greenland. Terrible because, as I understood it, it was preventable. But dealing with shame, preventing it, meant tackling it, and talking about it. Even if one could find and receive qualified help in the remote settlements and villages of Greenland, there was still no guarantee that talking about something would help. And thus, a so-called *simple* emotion, was elevated to something far more complex, just like the medical terms the doctors preferred.

But Serminnguaq had nothing to be ashamed

about, or did she?

"Arika," I said. "You vetted the applications, didn't you?"

"Yes. Most of them."

"And Shellenberger's?"

"Yes, but it was Lærke who wanted him on the expedition."

"Serminnguaq didn't apply, did she?"

"No, not formally."

"She was more of an afterthought…"

"That doesn't sound very complimentary, but you could, perhaps, call her that. She was added in the comments section of the application. Shellenberger called her his *companion*."

"And Lærke said that she was approved or *overseen* because you were all busy."

"And because she was already here. That's right."

I folded the letter into the diary and crawled to the entrance of the cave, leaning out as far as Arika would let me.

"Maratse," I said.

"*Iiji?*"

"I think I have something."

Maratse shone his light up towards me. My breath caught in my throat as the light glittered within a cone of blue-veined ice, twisting up towards me, before the light collected in the pockets of dimpled ice in the walls. I peered into the light, shielding my eyes with my hand. Serminnguaq was wearing the climbing harness, and I wondered how Maratse had convinced her to put it on? I deliberated for a moment, before calling down to them both in Danish, trusting that the latest from the diary would help ease Serminnguaq's mind.

"Josh Shellenberger had a heart problem," I said, my words echoing around the glassy walls. "He was born with it. Too much exertion, like walking across the ice in cold weather – it might have caused heart failure." The light from Maratse's torch flashed to Serminnguaq's head as he looked at her. I saw a measure of relief pass across her face, lifting her long cheeks for a moment, taking some of the weight, and hopefully erasing any guilt or responsibility she might have felt over Josh Shellenberger's death. "You didn't kill him, Serminnguaq," I said. "You didn't do it."

"But that's not why she ran, is it?" Arika said.

"No," I said, sliding back a little from the entrance to the cave. "I don't think so."

"But you have an idea?"

I did, but I wasn't sure I wanted to share it. I remembered Lærke saying she had seen Shellenberger and Serminnguaq holding hands. But she also said they often seemed to be fighting. I wondered how, if she couldn't speak English. I didn't imagine Shellenberger could speak Greenlandic, and I had not heard him speak Danish. So, unless Serminnguaq was lying about her languages, they would have been forced to communicate in other ways.

I looked up at Arika, as the sound of metal karabiners being screwed into harnesses clacked up the ice walls from the cave below.

"Imagine," I said, lowering my voice, "if a stranger came to your village."

"*My* village?"

"No, not yours. Here in Greenland."

"Okay…"

"Think about it. This man comes looking for you. He's your age. He has plenty of money – far more than you. And he says he wants to take you away with him."

"Are you asking me if I would go with him?" Arika shook her head. "Tell me this is hypothetical, before I shove your colonial arse through that hole."

"Sorry," I said, quickly, wondering if I really was cutting too fine a picture. "I mean Serminnguaq. Imagine she's twenty, and all she knows is what you've seen in the tiny settlements and villages. Then this man offers to take her away from all that."

"Where are you going with this?"

"What if she misunderstood?"

"Misunderstood?"

"She speaks no English. She's had the barest, most basic of educations, and this man whisks her away to America."

"You think Serminnguaq has been to America?"

"Josh took her," I said. "He must have."

"And?"

"And…" I let the word hang in the cold air between us, suddenly aware that I didn't want to finish that thought, not out loud. I didn't want to suggest that Serminnguaq had fallen in love with Josh, even though I was almost convinced that she had. I didn't want to say that she had misunderstood his familial longings for longings of another kind.

Without an interpreter, she would never have understood the excerpt of the diary he left for her in the village below Mount Dundas, only that a man had come looking for her. A rich man. A white man. Serminnguaq was orphaned the day her mother died, and again when her grandfather died. I couldn't begin to imagine how she would feel when her companion died on the ice at her feet, perhaps in the very spot, or at least close to the place where she had been conceived. Serminnguaq's turbulent life had come full circle, and she had sought refuge from the world, deep down under the ice.

"You never finished," Arika said.

"No, I didn't."

"What were you going to say?"

"I don't think it matters," I said. "Only today matters."

Arika frowned for a second, then shook it away as she grabbed the rope. She pointed at a belay device attached to an ice screw in the wall.

"I'll need help to pull them both up."

We pulled Serminnguaq up first. I took her hand as Arika grabbed her harness. Together we pulled her out of the cave and into the tunnel. She waited, sitting quietly, one hand grasped around the handrail screwed into the ice, while we pulled Maratse out of the cave. Arika made sure that everyone was secure, before instructing us to crawl out to the surface.

I lingered for a moment, squeezing the diary in my hands, glancing at Serminnguaq, until Maratse nudged me.

"What's wrong?" he said.

"Nothing. I'm just thinking." I opened the diary, checked that the wedding clipping was tucked safely inside the pages, and then wrapped the rubber bands around the diary. I gave the envelope with the doctor's letter to Maratse. "For the medical examiner," I said.

Maratse nodded as he tucked the envelope in a pocket inside his jacket. "What about that?" he said, with a nod at the diary.

"I was thinking about leaving it here," I said, lowering my voice. "All it is is trouble." I looked at Serminnguaq as Arika helped her into the tunnel. "But it's her family history, too."

"Hmm," Maratse said. "You read it."

"Yes."

"And you have a good memory?"

"It's not bad," I said. "I *am* a writer, you know."

"*Iiji*," he said. "Then you can write it down one day, for her, for Serminnguaq. But not today," he said, as he plucked the diary from my hands. "Today is for living, and recovering, and thinking about tomorrow."

"Yes," I said, as Maratse tossed the diary into the cave. It struck me that *today* will always be more important than *yesterday*, because it is the only day you can think about *tomorrow*.

Maratse grabbed his utility belt and nodded for me to crawl on ahead of him. I followed Serminnguaq out of the tunnel and onto the icecap. I studied her face, and behind the sad eyes I saw a hidden strength, wrapped around the light that reflected from the ice. There was a second when I thought I saw something, or someone reflected in Serminnguaq's eyes. A young woman perhaps, a little wild, but full of life and energy, twirling on the ice, waving at the exciting and strange young men as they drove across the icecap to build a city of the future beneath it. They left much in their wake, much of which would take hundreds or thousands of years to clean up and eradicate. But they left life too, and today was for living.

The End

Author's Note

While this novella will only give you a taste of the real story behind Camp Century, I hope it has whetted your interest to discover more. There are plenty of articles and videos on the Internet about the American secret base on the icecap, but I would also recommend the book *City under the Ice: The Story of Camp Century* by Charles Michael Daugherty, Macmillan, 1963. It reads like a wonderful bit of propaganda, but has some great details about a fascinating project.

As usual, I got a little carried away with the human aspect, and what could have occurred. When I lived in the far north of Greenland, I met people who said they could trace their genes back to some of the polar explorers who visited Greenland in the early days of exploration. It made for some interesting conversations, and, obviously, inspired this story.

However, while I have only hinted at the radioactive waste left behind as a result of the project, I do intend to return to this subject when I have more answers.

Chris
November 2019
Denmark

About the Author

Christoffer Petersen is the author's pen name. He lives in Denmark. Chris started writing stories about Greenland while teaching in Qaanaaq, the largest village in the very north of Greenland – the population peaked at 600 during the two years he lived there. Chris spent a total of seven years in Greenland, teaching in remote communities and at the Police Academy in the capital of Nuuk.

Chris continues to be inspired by the vast icy wilderness of the Arctic and his books have a common setting in the region, with a Scandinavian influence. He has also watched enough Bourne movies to no longer be surprised by the plot, but not enough to get bored.

You can find Chris in Denmark or online here:

www.christoffer-petersen.com

By the same Author

THE GREENLAND CRIME SERIES
featuring Constable David Maratse
SEVEN GRAVES, ONE WINTER Book 1
BLOOD FLOE Book 2
WE SHALL BE MONSTERS Book 3
INSIDE THE BEAR'S CAGE Book 4

Short Stories from the same series
KATABATIC
CONTAINER
TUPILAQ
THE LAST FLIGHT
THE HEART THAT WAS A WILD GARDEN
QIVITTOQ
THE THUNDER SPIRITS
ILULIAQ
SCRIMSHAW
ASIAQ
CAMP CENTURY
INUK
DARK CHRISTMAS
POSION BERRY

and

THE GREENLAND TRILOGY
featuring Konstabel Fenna Brongaard
THE ICE STAR Book 1

CHRISTOFFER PETERSEN

IN THE SHADOW OF THE MOUNTAIN Book 2
THE SHAMAN'S HOUSE Book 3

and

THE DARK ADVENT SERIES
featuring Police Commissioner Petra "Piitalaat" Jensen
THE CALENDAR MAN Book 1
THE TWELFTH NIGHT Book 2
and

THE POLARPOL ACTION THRILLERS
featuring Sergeant Petra "Piitalaat" Jensen *and more*
NORTHERN LIGHT Book 1
MOUNTAIN GHOST Book 2
WINTER BOUNTY Book 3

and

UNDERCOVER GREENLAND
introducing Inniki Rasmussen *and* Eko Simigaq
NARKOTIKA Book1

and

THE DETECTIVE FREJA HANSEN SERIES
set in Denmark and Scotland
FELL RUNNER Introductory novella
BLACKOUT INGÉNUE Book 1

and

MADE IN DENMARK
short stories featuring Milla Moth *set in Denmark*
DANISH DESIGN Story 1

and

THE WHEELMAN SHORTS
short stories featuring Noah Lee *set in Australia*
PULP DRIVER Story 1
and

THE WILD CRIME SERIES
featuring wildlife biologist Jon Østergård
set in Denmark and Alaska
PAINT THE DEVIL Book 1
LOST IN THE WOODS Book 2

and

GREENLAND NOIR (POETRY)
inspired by Seven Graves, One Winter & more
GREENLAND NOIR Volume 1

and

CONSTABLE MARATSE "STAND ALONE"
set in Greenland
ARCTIC STATE